MIRA
THE DETECTIVE

This hOle book belongs to

_____

Read more hOle books

MIRA
THE DETECTIVE

Pavithra Sankaran

Illustrations by Vandana Singh

duckbill

Duckbill Books and Publications Pvt Ltd
F2 Oyster Operaa, 35/36 Gangai Street Kalakshetra Colony,
Besant Nagar, Chennai 600090
www.duckbill.in
platypus@duckbill.in

First published by Duckbill Books 2018
Text copyright © Pavithra Sankaran 2018
Illustrations copyright © Vandana Singh 2018

This book was earlier published as *Something Fishy*

Pavithra Sankaran asserts the moral right to be identified
as the author of this work.

10 9 8 7 6 5 4 3 2

ISBN 978-93-83331-88-8

Typeset by PrePSol Enterprises Pvt. Ltd.

Printed at Thomson Press (India) Ltd.

Also available as an ebook

Children's reading levels vary widely. The general reading levels
are indicated by colour on the back cover. There are three levels:
younger readers, middle readers and young adult readers. Within
each level, the position of the dot indicates the reading complexity.
Books for young adults may contain some slightly mature material.

The Tic-Tic-Tic Trouble

The police! In her building! Mira was surprised and a bit afraid. The big policemen in their khaki uniforms always looked so strict, and every one of them had a paunch, exactly like PT Sir, who was very scary indeed.

Mira had never seen so many policemen in one place and most of them seemed to be standing outside HER MOTHER'S SHOP!

Someone put a hand on Mira's shoulder. She jumped.

Phew!
It was only Nambi
Uncle, the watchman.

'Come with me, child,'
Nambi Uncle said.

Normally Mira would
have retorted, 'I am not a
child! I am eight years old!' But
today she just followed him up the
stairs to her flat.

'Where is Amma? Why are there so

2

many policemen?' Mira could feel her tears gathering, but she did not cry. She set down her school bag, took off her shoes and put them neatly on the rack. She even picked her socks off the floor. She had never done this before, no matter how many times her mother yelled at her. But today she wanted to be good.

With all those policemen downstairs, it was better to be careful.

'There was a robbery in the shop last night.'

'Robbery! But how, Uncle? You are our watchman!' Mira loved Nambi Uncle with his giant moustache and small, bright eyes. She thought he was the strongest man in the world.

'We don't know how it happened. The police will find out. I have to go now, okay? Please close the door and lock it. Don't go anywhere till your mother comes. She told me to tell you, it is very *serious*.'

'Serious' was the word Amma used when she meant

it would be dangerous to disobey.

Mira did as she was told. She sat down on the sofa and began to think.

Mira loved her mother's small gems and antiques shop. It had such pretty things! They shone and sparkled and twinkled and flashed. It had strange old clocks and musical instruments that no one knew how to play. It also had platinum pens, emerald-encrusted keychains, solid silver cell phones and even a diamond-edged nailcutter. Mira loved looking at them whenever she went to the shop.

But most of all, she loved the large gold watch that was locked up inside a glass case. It was not for sale, Mira knew. It had been given to her grandfather by someone very important. It had a secret mechanism that made it run forever, without winding and without any batteries!

Mira suddenly wondered if the thief had taken it, too. That would be terrible!

'But, the camera! The CCTV camera inside the shop! It would have recorded everything. If we watch the video, we can find out who the thief is!' Mira jumped up, shouting excitedly. Excitement always made her shout. So, she did not hear the door open behind her.

'No, sweetheart, the police tried that,' said Mira's mother, walking into the house. 'The thief wore a mask, went up to the camera and threw a cloth over it. We can see nothing else in the video. There is only a TIC-TIC-TIC sound for a few minutes. Here, I have a recording on my phone.'

TIC-TIC-TIC went the recording. What would make a sound like that, wondered Mira. An animal? A clock? A BOMB? No, not a bomb. The police had checked the shop.

'Ma, has the thief taken everything? Even Grandpa's watch?' asked Mira worriedly.

'Only the watch, darling. It was the most valuable thing we had.'

Mira's face fell. So, it *was* gone.

But why did the thief take nothing else from a shop full of treasures? That was weird, thought Mira.

'Are you sad, Ma?'

Amma smiled, but tiredly. 'Yes, love, a little,' she said. 'Will you do me a favour, Mira? Will you go borrow a Crocin from Kamini Aunty? I have a headache.'

'Sure, Amma!' Mira said, turning towards the door.

'Remember to say please and thank you!' Amma called after her as she stepped out.

'Hello, my dear,' said a slow voice above Mira's head.

Mira knew Kamini Aunty
was a scientist but she did
not look like one. She didn't
wear glasses or a white coat.
She was tall and thin, and though she
always wore sneakers, she moved very
slowly. Rather like a camel, Mira often
thought. And she had long fingernails,
painted purple.

'Hello, Aunty,' Mira replied. 'Please,

do you have a Crocin?
Amma has a headache and
we don't have any at home.'

'Of course, she has a
headache, your poor, poor
mother. She shou-would
have one, wouldn't
she?' Kamini Aunty
said in her drawling
way. 'She must be
so *hassled*.'

Kamini Aunty
went inside and came
back with a pill.

As she took the pill from Kamini
Aunty's hand, Mira's eyes opened wide
in surprise. The purple nails! They were
gone! Chopped raggedly down to little
stubs!

Hurriedly, she said 'thank you',

and rushed back across the corridor. She had never seen Kamini Aunty without her long, bright, purple nails. And they were so badly cut! One nail even looked as if it was broken.

Even I can cut my own nails more neatly, and I am only eight, thought Mira.

Mira was dreaming of policemen playing football with purple cabbages, when the phone rang early next morning.

She heard her mother answer it.

'Gloves?' she heard her say. 'I see. Okay, I will come to the station right away.'

Mira suddenly remembered the theft. She sat up, just as Amma came into the room.

'Good morning, sweetheart. I have to go to the police station, so Nambi Uncle will come and be here for a while. I won't be long. Okay? I've kept your milk on the table. Don't forget to drink it.'

After her mother left, Mira switched on the TV. She was not supposed to do that, but Nambi Uncle was too busy with the newspaper to notice.

A while later, Nambi Uncle looked up. 'Your mother said the police have found a clue. They found one torn glove lying on the street. And there was a bit of a fingernail stuck to it.'

'Oh, the wicked thief!' cried Mira. 'He wore gloves so that he would not leave fingerprints!' She knew all about fingerprints and how the police used them to catch criminals, from a story she had read in school.

After two TV shows, Mira suddenly realised Amma would be back soon. She had better brush her teeth and drink the milk, or Amma would be very mad!

She switched off the
TV and was turning to go
when Nambi Uncle said,
'Mirakutty, do you have a
nailcutter?'

'Yes, I'll bring it,' said Mira. She
gave the nailcutter to Nambi Uncle
and went to the bathroom to brush
her teeth.

And just as she was squeezing
toothpaste onto the brush, she
heard it.

Tic Tic Tic Tic Tic Tic Tic Tic Tic Tic Tic Tic Tic Tic Tic

TIC-TIC-TIC.

The sound
she had heard
on Amma's
phone,
recorded from
the CCTV!

Mira's heart

pounded in fear.
Her hand shook so
much that the paste
dropped off the
toothbrush.

She stumbled out
of the bathroom and
suddenly knew what the
sound was. The nailcutter!
It was going TIC-TIC-TIC as
Nambi Uncle cut his nails!
All at once, she was very
afraid of him. She stepped back
and bolted herself into the bathroom.

Trying her best to make no noise,
Mira leaned against the bathroom wall
and wished dearly that her mother would
come back. She could still hear the
nailcutter.

She closed her eyes. Nails, nails.

Where had she seen nails recently? She could hear the TIC-TIC-TIC as the nail-cutter did its job. Cut nails … chopped nails … purple nails!

Mira opened her eyes wide.

She knew what the sound on the CCTV had been! It wasn't Nambi Uncle at all! She had to tell Amma. She had to tell the police. Even if the policemen looked like PT Sir, she would have to be brave and tell them.

She rushed out of the bathroom. 'Nambi Uncle! We have to go to Amma! Let us go to the police station!' she shouted.

'What happened?' Nambi Uncle jumped up.

Mira stopped and took a deep breath. She was shaking with fear and excitement.

'I know who stole the watch. I know the thief!' she whispered fiercely. She told him everything she had figured out.

Nambi Uncle lifted Mira up in one scoop, banged the door shut and leaped down the stairs. They zoomed off to the police station on his motorcycle.

At the police station, Mira ran to her mother.

'Mira! What are you doing here?' her mother exclaimed. 'What happened, Nambi?'

'Purple! It must have been a purple nail!' Mira shouted excitedly.

'What?' asked her mother.

'Was it? Was it? Was it purple? The bit of nail stuck in the glove?' asked Mira.

'It was, yes, but what ... how did you know?'

'I knew it! Kamini Aunty cut her nails in the shop, Amma! That was the TIC-TIC-TIC sound! Her purple nails are gone, Amma! She cut them hurriedly in the shop that's why they are so raggedy! She wore gloves to cover her fingerprints and, and her nails, they tore the gloves!' Mira burst out.

Exhibit 1A and 1B

'I have no idea what you are talking about. Why don't you sit down and tell me everything from the beginning?' said Mira's mother.

And so Mira did.

'If what you are saying is right, little girl, we must speak to Dr Kamini immediately,' said the police inspector.

Amma and Mira rode in a jeep, with the inspector and two other policemen, back to their building.

Amma and Mira went home, while the policemen marched up and knocked on Dr Kamini's door.

'You were perfectly right, little girl,' said the inspector.

Mira wished he would not call her a

'little girl'. In just five months she would be NINE!

'Dr Kamini has confessed. Just as you said, her long nails tore her gloves. She had a second pair, but she was afraid they would also tear, so she used the diamond-edged nailcutter in the shop to cut off her nails! When she was sneaking out of the shop, she dropped one of the gloves.'

'But why did she take only the watch? There are so many other pretty things in the shop.'

'Ah, the minds of scientists! She was only interested in the watch because of the secret mechanism that makes it run without stopping. She didn't want anything else. She wanted to find out what makes it tick.'

Congratulations
Dr Kamini!

'She asked me for the watch once,' Mira's mother added. 'But I refused to let anyone open it and take it apart. It's too precious.'

The policeman nodded.

'So, she decided to steal it. Anyway, Miss Mira, we must thank you very much for helping us.' He shook her hand and then saluted smartly.

Mira's mother smiled in pride.

NG NEWS - Dr Kamini wins the award for

As Mira shut the door behind the policemen, she heard her mother.

'You haven't drunk your milk, Mira! Come here and finish it right now!'

The Mayamix Mess

A moment before Mira poured her milk into the long-suffering pot of crotons, she noticed it looked different. She raised the mug of swirly pink milk and sniffed at it. Then she dipped a finger into the lukewarm liquid and sucked it.

Her eyes opened wide in delight. She gullugg-gullugg-gullugged the whole thing down in eight seconds flat.

And now, Mira, the

renowned milk-hater, wanted more.

'Sheila Aunty, can I have some more milk, please?' Mira's aunt was staying over while her mother travelled on work.

'Sure! But Leela said you were fussy about milk!' Sheila replied, going into the kitchen.

Mira followed her. 'When Amma gives me milk, it never tastes like this. It was so yummy! Like ... like warm ice cream! Did you put strawberries in it?'

Sheila Aunty laughed. 'No, no! All I put was this.'

And she held up a glittery pink box. It said MAYAMIX MALT in large rainbow-

coloured letters. Two fat, white-and-
pink bunnies sat on either side of the
rainbow, grinning widely. 'I found it in
the supermarket yesterday and thought
you might like it,' said Sheila Aunty.

'Amma makes me drink plain milk.' Mira made a face.

The Mayamix box sat on the kitchen counter and grew steadily lighter as Mira added two spoons to her mug, every morning and evening. Although Sheila Aunty had told her to put in only one.

A few days after Mira's aunt bought Mayamix, some people wearing bunny costumes came to her school and distributed little sachets of Mayamix Malt to the children.

From that day on, all the children in Mira's school were drinking it. And talking about it. And dreaming about it.

A week later, Mira's mother returned.

The next
morning,
a glass of
plain white
milk stood on the table.
Mira stood over it,
scowling.

'I don't want this!' she
said.

Somewhere behind her, a
croton winced.

'Please don't make me angry, Mira.
You know very well you don't have a
choice,' said her mother.

'I don't want, I don't want, I don't
want!' shouted Mira, stamping her foot.

'Listen, Mira. I will count to ten
and I want the milk finished before I'm
done.' Mira knew that tone very well. It
meant Trouble.

'I waaannnnt Mayamix!
I waaaant Maaayaaamiixxx,'
Mira wailed.

'You want *what*?' Mira's
mother was getting very impatient now.

'May ... Mayamix!' sobbed Mira.

'What is that?'

'It is ... it is a yummy powder to put
in the milk.' said Mira, still teary. 'Sheila
Aunty always let me put it! Only you
make me drink plain milk!'

'Mira, you know very well I don't
like these synthetic products. The sugar,
the preservatives, the additives, none of
them are good for you.'

'But everybody drinks Mayamix! I
waaant it, Amma, pleeeeease!'

'You drink this today, and then we'll
see,' replied Mira's mother.

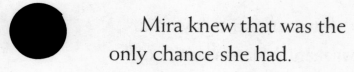

Mira knew that was the only chance she had.

Three minutes later, the croton looked distinctly relieved.

'HUNDREDS OF MAYAMIX BAGS VANDALISED, SUPPLIES DISRUPTED' said the headlines. Mira's mother was reading the paper out to her.

Over three hundred bags of the popular flavoured drink, Mayamix, were destroyed last night in a mystery break-in and attack at the company's factory not far from town. The supply of Mayamix to stores is likely to be affected. 'We will find out who is behind this and have them put away forever,' said a spokesperson for the company.

CityPaper

AFE SAVING
r the first time, an ar-
ificial heart that may
give patients up to five
years of extra life has
been successfully im-
planted in a 75-year-old
French man.

MAYAMIX MYSTERY
Over three hundred bags of the
popular flavoured drink mix,
Mayamix, were destroyed last
night in a mystery break-in and
attack at the company's factory
not far from town. The supply
of Mayamix to stores is likely
to be affected. 'We will find
out who is behind this and have
them put away forever,' said a
spokesperson for the company

The artificial heart, de-
signed by French bio-
medical firm Carmat, is
powered by Lithium-ion
batteries that can be
worn externally.

The artificial heart, de-
signed by French bio-
medical firm Carmat, is
powered by Lithium-ion
batteries that can be
worn externally.

For the first time, an at-
ificial heart that may
give patients up to five
years of extra life has
been successfully im-
planted in a 75-year-old
French man.

Mira's school was abuzz with the
news. Many children burst out crying
in the middle of lessons at the thought

of missing Mayamix for the next few weeks. The school had to be dismissed early because the teachers were grossed out at such a quantity of nose goo.

Mira thought about Mayamix so much that day, that she could bear it no longer. She ran most of the way home and dashed into the kitchen as soon as she'd taken off her shoes and socks. She rummaged in the cupboard and emerged clutching the old, empty Mayamix box. She put her hand in. There was a little bit of powder at the very bottom. Mira grabbed at it with her fingers.

The cardboard at the bottom of the box gave way. The pink powder fell to the ground. Mira stumbled forward in desperation and stepped right into the patch of Mayamix on the floor.

The powder stuck to her feet. She tried to scrape it off with her hands, but it stayed stuck. Feeling miserable, she hopped to the bathroom to wash it off. After five minutes of soaping and scrubbing, her hands and feet still looked rather rosy.

She came back to the kitchen to wipe the spilt Mayamix powder, and the mop turned pink, too. Mira began to get

a bit worried.
Amma would
certainly ask
questions
about this.

Mira was looking for Sunil, her best friend. He hadn't come to school that day and hadn't come out to play either. Sunil and Mira were the only two children in their building not allowed to drink Mayamix. Sunil's father was Nambi Uncle, the building watchman, and he said you could only become tall and strong if you drank plain milk with lots of cream floating in it.

Sunil's house was at the end of the compound, a little away from the apartment building. Mira knocked on the door. Sunil's mother opened it.

'Hello Aunty! Is Sunil at home? Why didn't he come to school? '

Sunil's mother was looking very worried. 'He is not well. He is resting and can't come out now.'

'Oh. Okay, Aunty, if he gets better, please tell him to come to my house.'

'Hmm, all right,' said Sunil's mother.

Mira went and sat on her favourite part of the compound wall just behind Sunil's house, where no one could see her. The clothesline was full of half-dry clothes, blowing gently in the breeze.

Mira's thoughts wandered back to Mayamix. She suddenly remembered Sunil's uncle, Tambi, was the watchman at the Mayamix factory! Why did Sunil have to fall ill now? There were so many things she wanted to ask him. He would

surely have heard from his uncle about the slashed bags.

A strong gust of wind blew away a shirt from the clothesline. Mira jumped down to get it. When she picked it up, she saw it had pink stains. It was Sunil's t-shirt.

She looked up at the other clothes

on the line. There was a pair of faded
blue pajamas that belonged to Sunil, also
with large pink patches. They looked just
like the pink patches made by Mayamix
on the mop at home. But Sunil's house
had no Mayamix because Nambi Uncle
would never buy it, so how did his
clothes become pink?

Mira's mind began whirring.

Mira stood on the compound wall and
clambered on to the window shade. She
walked carefully along it and then climbed
into the balcony to Sunil's room.

'Sunil! Sunil!' Mira called out in a
half-shout, half-whisper.

A face appeared. It
was very pink. Pink hands
opened the door and let
Maya into the room. Even his
toes were pink.

Maya started. This was very strange.
She put her hands out to show him

they were pink too! He first looked as if he might cry. Then he giggled.

'Did your uncle tell you about the Mayamix bags being slashed?' Mira had thought about her question carefully.

Sunil looked terrified. He said, 'If I tell you something, promise you won't tell anybody? God promise?'

Mira nodded solemnly.

'I went to stay with Tambi Uncle during the weekend. When I woke up at night to drink water, he was not there. The front door was open. I got scared and went to look for him. Then I heard a sound inside the Mayamix factory building. I peeped through the window and he was there with a torch and knife and he was tearing all the bags! I ran inside to stop him, but he pushed me away and I fell on the Mayamix powder.'

Sunil was nearly in tears. 'Amma and Appa are afraid someone will find out and send Tambi Uncle to jail. They are

not letting me go out of the house until the pink colour goes.'

Mira, her mother, Sunil, Nambi Uncle and his brother Tambi were sitting at the dining table in her house. Sheila Aunty was there, too. Mira's mother had called her over because she was a lawyer. Tambi Uncle looked terrified. He was twisting his fingers so much that Mira was convinced they would fall off.

They were all watching a video on Tambi Uncle's phone. It showed five men sitting around a table, talking.

'Our sales are not rising fast enough. We have to increase the Gluttonis in Mayamix.'

'But it will be dangerous to children's health if we increase it!'

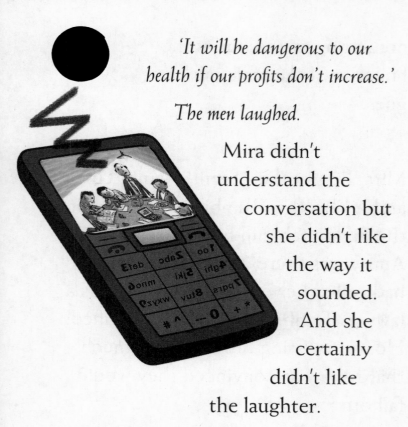

'It will be dangerous to our health if our profits don't increase.'

The men laughed.

Mira didn't understand the conversation but she didn't like the way it sounded. And she certainly didn't like the laughter.

Mira's mother turned to the children. 'Gluttonis is a chemical that makes you want more of whatever you are eating. It makes you *addicted*, which means you cannot stop wanting it. It is also bad for health. Mayamix has a lot of it. And these people were planning to put even more

of it in the powder. So that
children would drink more
Mayamix and the company
would make more money.'

Mira remembered the two spoonfuls
and felt her ears burning.

'I couldn't let them do it! I just
couldn't!' Tambi Uncle buried his head
in his hands.

'Aunty, please don't let the police
take Tambi Uncle away.' Sunil looked as
if he might cry.

'Don't worry Sunil, we won't,' said Sheila Aunty, eyes flashing. 'Not while I am around. And it was a very good thing you did, recording the Mayamix officers' conversation on your phone, Tambi.'

The doorbell rang. The police inspector and two constables stood there.

'Come in, sir,' Sheila Aunty said. 'We have something to show you.'

'COURT ORDERS MAYAMIX FACTORY CLOSED.'

Mira read the headlines. She asked her mother to read out the rest.

A local court has ordered that the Mayamix factory be closed and the product be withdrawn from shops immediately. The order came after tests

that showed the popular milk mix
contained an addictive substance,
Gluttonis, known to be harmful.
The court may also convict the owners
of the factory following a video showing that they
knew the substance was dangerous.

Mira's mother looked at her. Mira looked at the calm, white, liquid in her mug and sighed. Visions of a pink, frothy, creamy, luscious drink floated in front of her. She picked up the mug, closed her eyes and went gullugg-gullugg-gullug. There! It was done.

The croton put out a new leaf.

The Payasam Puzzle

Mira and her friends, Sunil and Laya, staggered home, looking ragged, dirty and tired. School would reopen in a few days, and they were making sure not a single minute of the holidays got away. They had been police and robbers, they had scraped their knees rebuilding piles of seven stones and they had yelled themselves hoarse cheering on a dog race between Boondi and Haali, the strays that lived outside their building.

The unmistakeable
aroma of Mrs Anita Varma's
coconut, cardamom and
prshprshprsh payasam wafted
around them and made their mouths
water.

'Amma, did Anita Aunty give us
some payasam?' Mira asked her mother.

Anita Aunty always distributed
generous amounts of the payasam to all
her neighbours.

'Hmm, no, darling. Why don't you
all wash up? And then you can have the

mango milkshake that's in the fridge,' said Mira's mother, looking up from her files and papers.

A few minutes later, they all had yellow milkshake moustaches. But Sunil sighed.

'I can't stop thinking about Anita Aunty's payasam. Do you think she'll give us some?'

'She always does, just wait,' replied Mira.

'Okay, let's go peep and see if it is ready,' said Laya. 'If Anita Aunty sees us, she might give us some right away.'

They all trooped upstairs. The door to Mrs Varma's house was wide open. The children peeped in. No one seemed to be home, but the fragrance of the payasam filled the air and their nostrils. Sunil groaned.

'Where is Anita Aunty?' Mira wondered.

Anita Aunty never left her front door open. She locked it carefully even when she went to gather clothes hung up to dry on the terrace.

Sunil could take it no longer. Throwing aside all caution, he dashed into the kitchen. It was empty. He looked all over for the payasam, but it was nowhere to be seen.

'Has she taken it to distribute?'

But Mira couldn't help feeling that there was something fishy about it all. Where was Anita Aunty?

'She must have gone to buy some of that secret payasam ingredient, *prshprshprsh*,' Mira's mother said. 'Not everything is a mystery, Mira!'

But when Anita Aunty had not turned up by the next morning, the whole building was worried. Mira's mother went

to the police station to lodge
a missing person complaint.
She came back looking rather
anxious.

'A person has to be missing for more
than two days, only then will the police
take a complaint,' Mira's mother told her.
'We will have to wait until tomorrow.'

That evening, Mira sat alone on
the building compound wall, trying to
think of where Anita Aunty could have
gone. Her mother had telephoned Anita
Aunty's son, but no one had answered
the phone. The coconut, cardamom and
prshprshprsh payasam kept coming into her
mind, not letting her think.

Suddenly, she realised the smell
was for real! The payasam aroma was in
the air. Nothing else in the world smelt
anything like it.

She jumped off the wall and rushed
up the stairs to Anita Aunty's apartment.
But it was locked, with the lock Nambi
Uncle had put on the door. She rang
the bell, just in case. No one answered.
Clearly, nobody was home.

And the payasam
fragrance was fainter, too.
Mira could barely smell it
here. She ran back down the
stairs. Ah, the aroma was back. Where
was it coming from?

'Sunil, come with me!' Mira hissed
at her sleeping friend, tugging at his
sleeve. Sunil was napping and his
mother was watching the news. The
only person who could follow the
payasam aroma like a bloodhound was
Sunil. She needed him.

When she had managed to get him
out of bed and to the compound wall,
the smell was still there, but less strong.

'We have to find out where it is coming
from. Anita Aunty is the only person who
knows how to make it,' said Mira.

Sunil closed his eyes and sniffed. Then he pointed. Over the wall!

'What? That's the Ruchi people's house!' Mira exclaimed.

The new neighbours in the house across the wall owned a restaurant called Ruchi. None of the children had ever been there, but Mira's mother sometimes ordered their yummy biryani.

Sunil nodded, with his eyes still closed. He could smell better that way.

'Are you sure?' asked Mira.

Sunil nodded again impatiently.

'Okay, okay!' said Mira.

'But why would the smell come from the Ruchi people's house? What is it doing there? And where is Anita Aunty anyway?'

Sunil was hungry and still sleepy. He said drowsily, 'Maybe they wanted her

payasam and she refused to give it to them, so they stole it. I know I'd steal it if she refused to give it to me.'

Mira gasped. Sunil might be on the right track! But a payasam stolen yesterday wouldn't smell so good today. Perhaps Anita Aunty was in the Ruchi people's house, making the payasam. But why would she go there without telling anyone? And without locking her house? Was she ... was she ... kidnapped?!

She grabbed Sunil's arm. 'We have to go find her! If she isn't in the Ruchi people's house, where did the payasam smell come from? We must rescue Aunty before they do anything bad to her. Let's go find her!'

'NOW?!' Sunil was suddenly wide awake. The sun had set and it was

already dark. He didn't think much of Mira's idea of finding Anita Aunty at this hour.

'I am going. Don't come if you don't want to, scaredy cat!' retorted Mira.

Sunil sighed and followed her.

Mira crept closer and closer to the

Ruchi house, along the hedge. Some of the plants had thorns. Her arms were getting scratched. She was really scared, but she couldn't turn back after what she had said to Sunil.

They were very close to the house now. Mira crept up and tried to peep through a window. She could see nothing.

She decided to try the back door. She look around to make sure no one was watching and tried the handle; it wouldn't budge.

Sunil suddenly whispered, 'Look, that window is partly open!'

She looked to her right and saw he was right. But it seemed too high off the ground for them to reach.

'How will we reach it?'
she asked.

But Sunil had thought of
that—he crouched on all fours
and whispered to Mira that she should
climb on his back. She took off her
slippers and stepped on his back. Sunil
groaned under his breath. She pulled at

the window; it opened with a loud creak.

Mira found herself looking into a kitchen. The payasam aroma was so strong, Mira could hardly breathe. As her eyes adjusted to the darkness, she saw something in the corner. It looked like a large cloth bundle ... No! It was Anita Aunty! She was tied to a chair and she seemed to have fainted!

Mira had seen enough. She was completely terrified. If the Ruchi people caught them, they would be kidnapped and taken away too!

She got down in a hurry, and dragged Sunil back to the hedge. Just then, a car turned into the gate.

The headlights swept through the hedge. Any second now, they would be

seen! Sunil pushed Mira to the ground.
They both lay absolutely flat, their hearts
hammering away in terror. The light
passed inches above them.

The car drove into the garage. The
two children scrambled up and ran for
their lives.

Mira and Sunil burst into her house, just as her mother was leaving for the police station. The two of them had not been seen since seven o'clock and their parents had been looking for them frantically.

'Mira! Where were you? What is the matter with you two! Do you have any

idea how worried we were?'
Mira's mother was angrier than
they had ever seen her.

Sunil's mother suddenly
noticed how ragged the children looked.
'What have you been doing? Your
clothes are all torn and your arms are
bleeding!'

Suddenly, the parents were all
concern. 'Are you all right? Come here.
Oh, that gash looks terrible!'

Mira burst out, 'Amma! No, my
arm doesn't hurt! Anita Aunty has been
kidnapped by the Ruchi people! They
have tied her up in their kitchen. We
think they want her payasam! We have
to rescue Anita Aunty!'

Mira's mother had no idea what they
were talking about, but she knew her
daughter enough to know there would

be some sense to the story later. At the word 'kidnap' she had already begun calling the police.

'They wanted the recipe, but Mrs Varma would not give it to them, so they got very angry and decided to kidnap her and force her to reveal it. You see, their restaurant had been doing very badly of late, and they thought something as magical as Mrs Varma's payasam would be exactly the thing to bring their customers back.' The police inspector was sitting in Mira's house the next morning, sipping some tea. 'But tell me, is it as wonderful as all of you say it is? Good enough to kidnap someone for? All for a payasam?'

Just then, they smelt it again. Mira and Sunil looked at each other.

'What is that incredible fragrance?' The police inspector was sniffing the air like a hound on a trail.

The children's faces broke out in huge smiles. The aroma grew stronger and stronger.

'Here you all are! I am so sorry, I didn't have enough cardamom, and the tender coconut was not so tender any more, you know, it has been sitting in my kitchen for three days. It is best made with freshly-plucked ones, of course.' Anita Aunty bustled into Mira's house, carrying an enormous vessel, and talking all the time.

The inspector got up and followed her,

without realising what he was doing. He snatched the lid off and inhaled deeply. Then he grabbed a spoon, dipped it in and slurped up the tender coconut, cardamom and *prshprshprsh* payasam.

He closed his eyes. 'Ahhh! No wonder they stooped to kidnapping! Who wouldn't!'

Pavithra Sankaran grew up a gluttonous reader and, according to people who have to live with her, she continues to be one. She reads everything, even the crumpled, oily newspapers roadside bajjis are wrapped in. She also eats nearly anything and almost always wants more. She likes trees, animals and slightly mad people. She lives in a house where toothbrushes, combs and shoes that belong to no one keep appearing at regular intervals.

A dreamer and a drawer Vandana Singh trained to be a pilot, a sculptor and became a film maker! A passionate animal lover, she worked at WWF India for six years and currently lives in Delhi and works as a freelance illustrator and designer.